MY
CAT STORY

ELLIOTT GILBERT

To order additional copies of this book, contact:
Xlibris
844-714-8691
www.Xlibris.com
Orders@Xlibris.com

ISBN: Softcover   978-1-6698-0294-5
          Hardcover   978-1-6698-0295-2
          EBook   978-1-6698-0296-9

Library of Congress Control Number: 2021952301

Print information available on the last page.

Rev. date: 12/07/2021

MY CAT STORY

Elliott Gibber

A CAT STORY

3

MY CAT

Told in Pictures

STORY

by ELLIOTT GILBERT

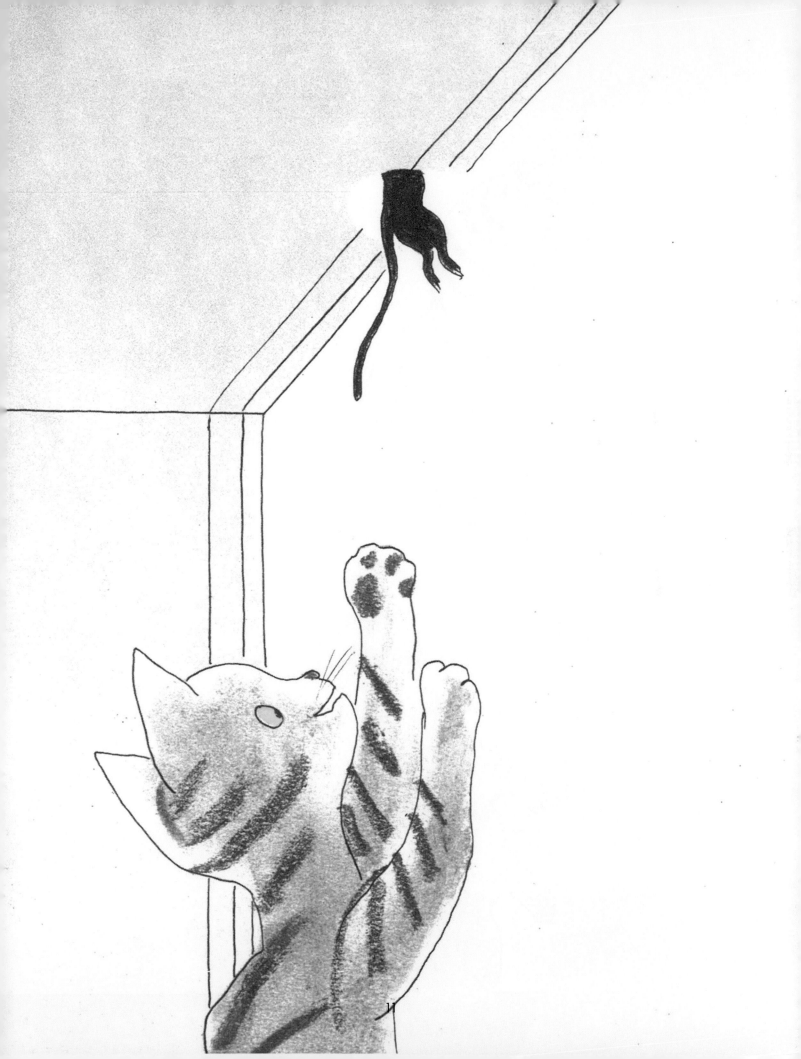

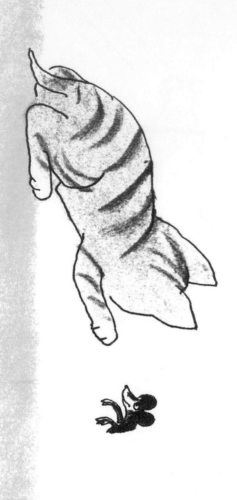

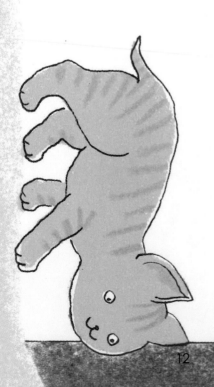

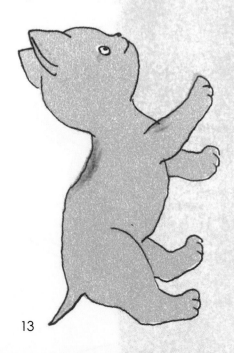

14

24

25

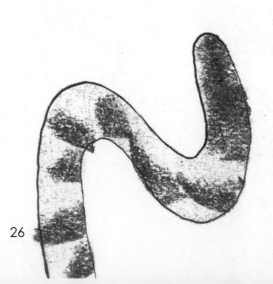

26

29

32